BOO BOOKS

HAIR SCARE!

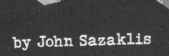

by John Sazaklis

illustrated by Patrycja Fabicka

PICTURE WINDOW BOOKS
a capstone imprint

Published by Picture Window Books
an imprint of Capstone
1710 Roe Crest Drive
North Mankato, Minnesota 56003
capstonepub.com

Library of Congress Cataloging-in-Publication Data
Names: Sazaklis, John, author. | Fabicka, Patrycja, illustrator.
Title: Hair scare! / by John Sazaklis ; illustrated by Patrycja Fabicka.
Description: North Mankato, Minnesota : Picture Window Books,
[2023] | Series: Boo books | Audience: Ages 5-7. | Audience: Grades
K-1. | Summary: Hattie finds brushing her hair an annoying problem
because it gets tangled, but when her Hairy Godfather changes
her hair to snakes she discovers that some things are much bigger
problems then hair tangles.
Identifiers: LCCN 2021970045 (print) | LCCN 2021058778 (ebook) |
ISBN 9781666339963 (hardcover) | ISBN 9781666340020 (pdf) | ISBN
9781666340044 (kindle edition) Subjects: LCSH: Snakes—Juvenile
fiction. | Hairdressing—Juvenile fiction. | Horror tales. | Humorous
stories. | CYAC: Hairdressing—Fiction. | Snakes—Fiction. | Horror
stories. | Humorous stories. | LCGFT: Horror fiction. | Humorous fiction.
| Picture books. Classification: LCC PZ7.S27587 Hai 2023 (print) | LCC
PZ7.S27587 (ebook) | DDC 813.6 [E]—dc23/eng/20220111
LC record available at https://lccn.loc.gov/2021970045
LC ebook record available at https://lccn.loc.gov/2021970108

Designer Nathan Gassman

Printed and bound in the USA. 4882

TABLE OF
CONTENTS

CHAPTER ONE
BAD HAIR DAY

"Rise and shine, Hattie!" said Mom. "Time to get moving!"

I pulled the covers over my head. *Why is school so early? Why can't I just skip it once in a while?*

Mom pulled the covers off and said, "Hurry up, or you'll be late for school!"

I dressed myself and looked in
the mirror. There was a big, bushy
bird's nest on top of my head.

"You better brush that hair,
young lady," Mom called. "It's
out of control."

"No thanks!" I yelled back.

I've tried brushing my hair before. Really, I have! It's just that I lose brushes that way. There are too many tangles and even more knots. I've tried everything. Nothing works. So that's that. It is what it is.

"I don't care about my stupid hair!" I yelled angrily.

Suddenly—POOF!—my room filled with colorful smoke.

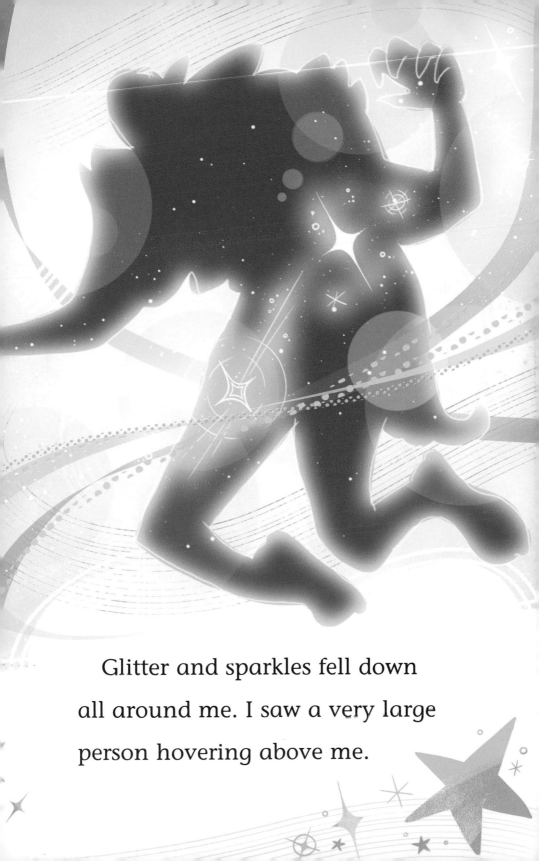

Glitter and sparkles fell down
all around me. I saw a very large
person hovering above me.

"What is going on?" I asked.
"Who *are* you?"

The scary stranger floated right toward me.

"I'm your Hairy Godfather!" he boomed in a loud voice. "And I don't like what I hear."

The magical fairy wuved his wand and said, "Hair today, gone tomorrow!"

Lightning flashed and thunder rumbled. KA-KOOM!

All of a sudden, my head was covered in slithering snakes!

CHAPTER TWO

HATS OFF, HATTIE!

"AAAAAAAHH!" I screamed. "What did you do to me?"

"I fixed your problem," he said. "Now you don't have to brush your hair. You just need to feed it!"

"What am I supposed to feed snakes?" I shrieked.

"Snake snacks, of course," the Hairy Godfather replied. Then he disappeared.

POOF!

The wriggling reptiles crawled
onto my face. Their silky skin
tickled my cheeks.

"Stop it!" I yelled. "Stay still!"

"Hattie!" Mom called. "The bus
is here!"

How was I going to get out of
this magical mess?

Aha! I found a thick winter hat
with flaps. I quickly covered my
head and ran to the bus.

CHAPTER THREE
HISSY FIT

I sat all the way in the back of the bus, trying not to be seen.

"Hey Hattie! What's with the hat?" asked my friend Athena.

"What hat?" I said.

HISSSSSSSSSS!

"The hissing hat on your head,"
said Athena. "That wiggling winter
one you're wearing on the hottest
day of the year."

I started to sweat from the heat
and the fear.

Suddenly, the snakes chewed
through the hat. They were hungry!
Athena was horrified. She
screamed. The other kids on the
bus saw the snakes and they
screamed too!

The driver slammed on the brakes.

SCREEEEEEECH!

"What's going on back there?"
the driver asked.

"Nothing!" I yelled. "I'm just having a bad hair day!"

I grabbed the snakes in a tight grip, but I could not control them. They dragged me out of my seat. They chomped and chewed on everything in sight.

My classmates climbed over their seats. They were trapped . . . and soon to be snake snacks!

"I wish I had my hair back,"
I cried.

POOF!

My Hairy Godfather appeared,
holding his magic wand.

"Snake, rattle, and roll!"
he boomed.

There was an explosion of glitter and sparkles.

BOOM!

Instantly, the creepy crawlies changed back into my regular hair. Only now, it was smooth and free of knots.

"Thank you!" I said with joyful tears. "I promise to brush my hair from now on."

"If you don't take care, you're in for another scare!" said the Hairy Godfather as he flew away with graceful speed.

I sat back in my seat. Athena stared at me.

"What was *that* about?" she asked.

"Forget it," I said. "That hair-raising horror is hiss-tory."

AUTHOR

John Sazaklis is a *New York Times* bestselling author with almost 100 children's books under his utility belt! He has also illustrated Spider-Man books, created toys for *MAD* magazine, and written for the BEN 10 animated series. John lives in New York City with his superpowered wife and daughter.

ILLUSTRATOR

Patrycja Fabicka is an illustrator with a love for magic, nature, soft colors, and storytelling. Creating cute and colorful illustrations is something that warms her heart— even during cold winter nights. She hopes that her artwork will inspire children, as she was once inspired by *The Snow Queen, Cinderella,* and other fairy tales.

bushy (BOOSH-ee)—thick and fluffy

chomp (CHOMP)—to make small waves

hover (HUHV-ur)—to remain in one place in the air

wriggle (RIG-uhl)—to quickly move up and down

DISCUSSION QUESTIONS

1. How do you think Hattie's mom felt about Hattie never combing her hair?

2. Were you surprised when Hattie's hair turned into snakes? What else could it have turned into?

3. What would you have done if you were on the bus with Hattie and the snakes?

WRITING PROMPTS

1. Make a list of three things Hattie could do to take care of her hair better.

2. Write a paragraph about what you would wish for if a fairy godfather or godmother showed up.

3. Pretend you are Athena. Write a journal entry about your friend and her bad hair day.

SCARED SILLY JOKES!

How do hair stylists work faster?
They take short cuts.

What do monsters put in their hair?
scare spray

Where do pirates go to get their hair cut?
The barrrrrber shop.

What kind of hair do you find at the beach?
wavy

What makes music on your hair?
a headband

Where does a sheep get a haircut?
The baa baa shop.

Why do bees have sticky hair?
Because they use honey combs.

What is a bees favorite hair style?
a buzz cut

BOO BOOKS

Discover these just-right frights!

Only from Capstone